The
Dinosaurs'
Last Days

Dr. Alvin Granowsky

RSVP
RAINTREE
STECK-VAUGHN
P U B L I S H E R S
The Steck-Vaughn Company

Austin, Texas

Illustrations by
Paul Lopez

Many scientists have tried to solve the mystery
of what happened to the dinosaurs.
They have made one guess after another.
So far, none of these guesses
has been proved true.

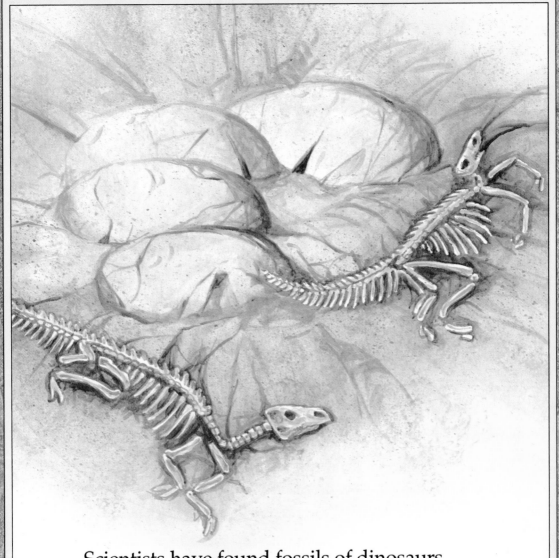

Scientists have found fossils of dinosaurs.
A fossil is what is left of an animal
that died long ago.
Dinosaur fossils are often found in small pieces.
It can take hundreds of hours to put the fossil
pieces together.

All that scientists know about dinosaurs they
have learned by studying fossils
and asking questions.
Clues in the fossils help scientists find answers
to their questions about dinosaurs.

Scientists have used fossil clues to guess
how different dinosaurs looked and
how dinosaurs lived.

5

Scientists wondered how dinosaurs were born.
When fossils of dinosaur nests were found,
scientists discovered that some dinosaurs
hatched from eggs.

Scientists compared the dinosaur eggs to the eggs of animals that are alive today.

This fossil of a Maiasaura egg is as long as three alligator eggs.

Studying egg fossils helped scientists learn more about the Maiasaura.

Fossils showed that the baby dinosaur that
hatched from the Maiasaura egg was a foot long.

8

Scientists wondered what happened
after the baby dinosaur hatched.

9

Some scientists guessed that baby dinosaurs could take care of themselves as soon as they hatched.

But fossil finds showed that some mother
dinosaurs stayed with their babies.

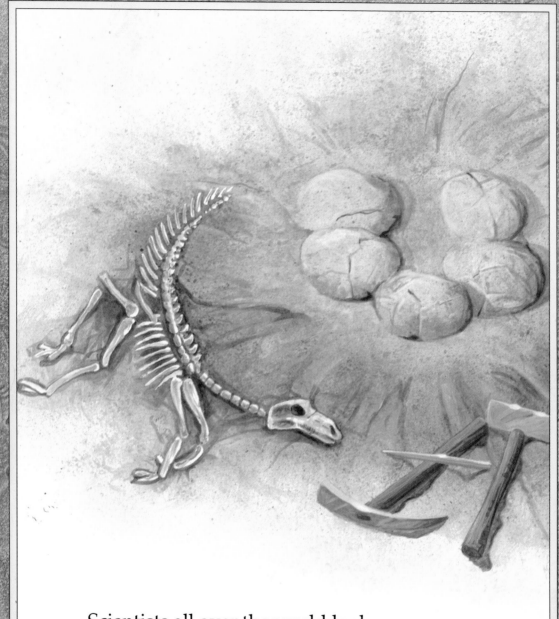

Scientists all over the world look
for dinosaur fossils.
Whenever new fossils are found, scientists study
the fossils for clues about dinosaur life.

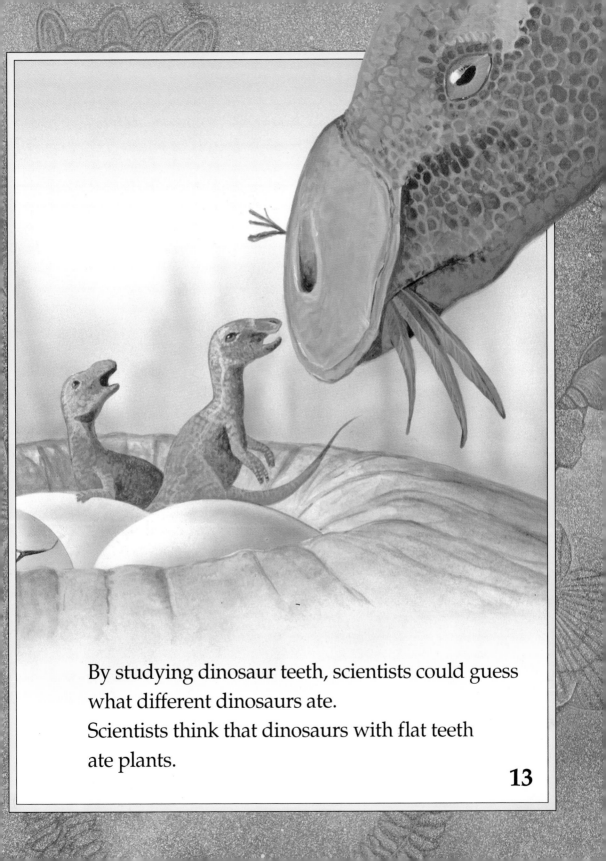

By studying dinosaur teeth, scientists could guess what different dinosaurs ate.
Scientists think that dinosaurs with flat teeth ate plants.

Scientists found the fossils of several adult
dinosaurs near nests of babies.
These fossils made scientists think that some
dinosaurs worked together to protect their babies.

14

Scientists have helped us learn many interesting
things about dinosaur life.
We know what some dinosaurs looked like.
We know where they lived and what they ate.
We even know how some dinosaur babies lived.

But all that we know about dinosaur life does not explain why there are no dinosaurs alive today.

By comparing fossils all over Earth,
scientists have discovered
when the last dinosaurs lived.

17

Until about 65 million years ago many dinosaurs
walked on Earth.
Scientists know this from the age of the rocks
in which dinosaur fossils were found.

18

But in layers of rock that formed later,
there are no dinosaur fossils.
Something happened to the dinosaurs.
But what happened?

Something killed off the dinosaurs.
It is hard to imagine what could kill animals
as big as the Saltasaurus.

20

What could destroy animals as fierce and strong
as the Tyrannosaurus?

Even dinosaurs with special protection died out.
The Triceratops had huge horns.
The Stegosaurus had a powerful tail.

The Ankylosaurus was covered with armor.
But all of these dinosaurs disappeared.
What happened to the dinosaurs?

Scientists do not know.
They look for clues in the fossils they find.
Fossil clues help scientists guess
why the dinosaurs became extinct.

24

Maybe there were great floods.
Could floods have killed the dinosaurs?

Some scientists think that a giant meteorite
hit Earth.
Clouds of dust from a meteorite
could block the sun's light.
Without the sun, plants and animals would die.

26

Many volcanoes were part of Earth at the time dinosaurs lived.
Maybe dark clouds of ash and dust from volcanoes killed the dinosaurs.

Some scientists wonder if Earth's climate
changed during the dinosaurs' last days.
Maybe the weather turned very cold
and many of the plants died.

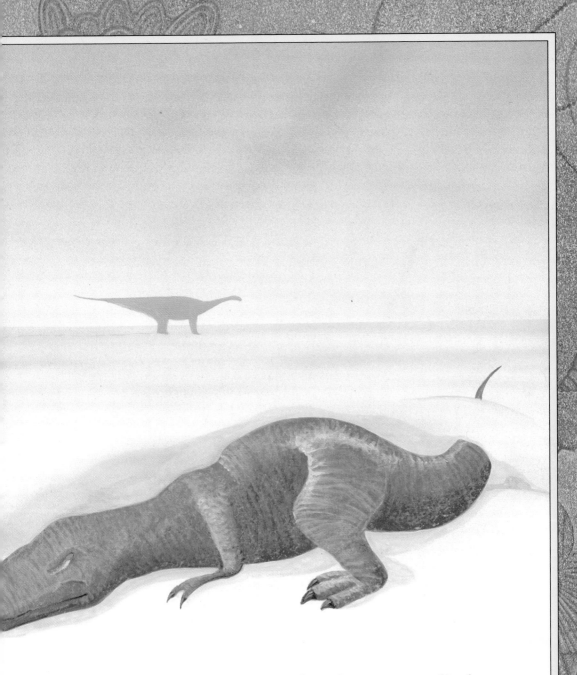

Without enough plants to eat, the plant-eaters died.
When the plant-eaters were gone,
the meat-eaters had nothing to eat and they died.

Maybe a terrible disease spread among the
dinosaurs and they grew sick and died.

There may be more than one reason
the dinosaurs became extinct.
Scientists don't know for sure.

No one knows what happened to the dinosaurs.
Scientists are still trying to find out.
For now, it is a mystery!

Look for these animals in
▬ The Dinosaurs' Last Days ▬

Ankylosaurus
(an KY luh sawr uhs)
18, 22, **23**

Pteranodon
(tehr AN uh dahn)
17

Stenonychosaurus
(sten oh nike uh SAWR uhs)
26

Corythosaurus
(kuh rith uh SAWR uhs)
24

Saltasaurus
(sahl tuh SAWR uhs)
20, 20, **25**, **32**

Triceratops
(try SEHR uh tahps)
17-18, **22**, 22, **27**

Maiasaura
(my uh SAWR uh)
1-2, **4-6**, 7-8, **10-11**, **13**,
14-15, **16**, **18**, **25**, 28, 30-31

Stegosaurus
(stehg uh SAWR uhs)
22, 22, **27**, **31**

Tyrannosaurus
(tih ran uh SAWR uhs)
21, 21, 29

Boldface type indicates that the animal appears in an illustration.

Acknowledgments
Design and Production: Design Five, N.Y.
Illustrations: Paul Lopez
Line Art: John Harrison

Staff Credits
Executive Editor: Elizabeth Strauss
Project Editor: Becky Ward
Project Manager: Sharon Golden

Trade Edition published 1992 © Steck-Vaughn Company

Library of Congress Cataloging-in-Publication Data

Granowsky, Alvin, 1936–
   The dinosaurs' last days / written by Alvin Granowsky: illustrated by Paul Lopez.
     p. cm.—(World of dinosaurs)
   Summary: Examines various scientific theories about the extinction of the dinosaurs, involving floods, giant meteorites, cold weather, disease, and simultaneous volcanic eruptions.
   ISBN 0-8114-6225-0
   1. Dinosaurs—Juvenile literature. 2. Extinction (Biology)—Juvenile literature.
[1. Dinosaurs. 2. Extinction (Biology)] I. Lopez, Paul, ill. II. Title. III. Series.
QE862.D5G7323   1992
567.9'1—dc20   91-23408
                                                     CIP AC

ISBN 0-8114-3250-5 Hardcover Library Binding
ISBN 0-8114-6225-0 Softcover Binding

3 4 5 6 7 8 9 LB 96 95